THE LEAGUE OF ENCHANTED HEROES

BY
TIM COLLINS &
JAMES LAWRENCE

Badger Publishing Limited
Oldmedow Road,
Hardwick Industrial Estate,
King's Lynn PE30 4JJ

Badger
LEARNING

Telephone**: 01438 791037**
www.badgerlearning.co.uk

2 4 6 8 10 9 7 5 3

The League of Enchanted Heroes
ISBN 978-1-78464-524-3

Text © Tim Collins 2016
Complete work © Badger Publishing Limited 2016

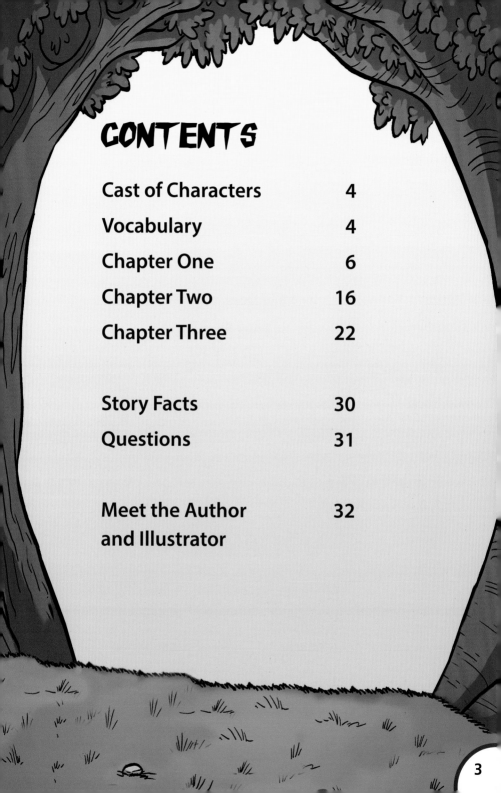

CONTENTS

CHARACTERS

JACK

HANSEL AND GRETEL

RED RIDING HOOD

RAPUNZEL

TOM THUMB

VOCABULARY

beanstalk	enchanted
combing	genius
curious	hooded
crumbling	lasso
emerged	replaced

Once Upon

Another

A

Time...

CHAPTER ONE
INTO THE WOODS

"Are you Jack?"

A girl in a bright red hooded top was standing in the alleyway.

Jack nodded.

"We need your help," said the girl. "Follow me."

She sprinted down the alley.

Jack was too curious to resist. He ran after her.

Jack followed the girl into the woods at the edge of town.

They passed through a faded door in a crumbling stone wall. On the other side, the trees were thicker and darker.

As he ran after the girl, Jack noticed her top had been replaced by a long, red cape.

They stopped in the middle of a wide clearing.

"I've found him," shouted the girl.

Four figures emerged from the gloomy forest.

"This is Rapunzel, Tom Thumb, Hansel and Gretel," said the girl. "Welcome to our league, Jack the Giant Killer."

"Giant Killer?" asked Jack. "You've got it wrong. I've never killed any giants."

"Well that's just great," said Tom Thumb, folding his arms across his chest. "Another stroke of genius from Little Red Riding Hood. We ask for Jack the Giant Killer and she brings us Jack the Giant Loser. It's times like this I wish the Big Bad Wolf had won."

"Give him a chance," said Rapunzel, who was combing her long, blonde hair. "He might still be able to help us."

"So what are your powers?" asked Gretel. "Can you do this?"

She held her hands out and shut her eyes. Bright blue flames rose from her palms.

"Or this?" asked Hansel.

He took a catapult out of his pocket and shot a gobstopper into the air at rapid speed.

"Didn't anyone tell you sweets are bad for you?" he asked. "That's the line I use when I've beaten a villain."

"We don't get to hear it very often," muttered Tom Thumb.

CHAPTER TWO
GIANT ATTACK

There was a heavy stomping in the woods.

Trees snapped and toppled over.

Jack gasped as he saw the dark shape of a giant lumbering towards them.

He scrabbled back as a foot as large as a car slammed into the clearing.

"There you all are. Just in time for lunch!" roared the giant.

"Enchanted heroes assemble!" shouted Tom Thumb.

He leapt up and threw himself on the giant's big toe.

The creature let out a deep yelp of pain and grabbed its foot. It hopped around, sending small earthquakes through the clearing.

Rapunzel grabbed a length of her hair and tied it into a lasso. She threw it around the end of the creature's foot and yanked it.

The giant crashed to the ground, sending up a massive cloud of dust.

Hansel fired gobstoppers at the fallen giant.

Gretel shot blue balls of flame.

But it was no use. The creature got back to its feet.

CHAPTER THREE
JACK VERSUS THE GIANT

Jack felt a shape in his back pocket. His chewing gum had been replaced by something bulky.

He pulled it out. A bag of multi-coloured beans!

He threw one on the ground and watched a thick beanstalk shoot into the sky.

Jack clambered up the beanstalk. He'd never even climbed a tree before but he had no problem leaping around the twisting vines.

The giant roared and raced up after him, making the beanstalk sway violently.

Near the top, Jack could see a long stem stretching out.

He ran across it, trying not to glance at the treetops far below.

The giant grabbed at him.

A bright blue flash lit up the sky. Gretel had flown to the top of the beanstalk too. She fired a ball of flame into the giant's back.

It slipped and fell, but grabbed the stem on the way down.

Jack ran back towards the giant. Its huge hand was straining to hold on. Jack kicked it as hard as he could.

The giant's hand slid away and it fell down to the ground.

With the weight gone, the stem sprung up like a big catapult, flinging Jack into the air.

Jack was falling. The world was a sick, dizzy blur.
He was sure he was about to splat into the forest floor.
But, rather than solid earth, he struck something soft.

He'd landed in the middle of Red Riding Hood's cloak.
She had stretched it out to break his fall with help
from Hansel, Rapunzel and Tom Thumb.

They lowered Jack to the ground. The lifeless body
of the giant was lying behind them.

"Looks like you really are a giant killer," said Red
Riding Hood. "Welcome to the League of Enchanted
Heroes."

STORY FACTS

This story brings together characters from five different fairy tales – *Jack and the Beanstalk*, *Hansel and Gretel*, *Little Red Riding Hood*, *Rapunzel* and *Tom Thumb*.

Jack and the Beanstalk was first published over 200 years ago. In the original story, Jack climbs a beanstalk, visits a castle and steals treasure from a giant. Then he chops down the beanstalk with an axe, causing the giant to fall to his death. Some later versions change the story so Jack is getting revenge for his father's death.

The characters in this story work together like superhero teams such as *The Justice League of America*, *The Guardians of the Galaxy* and *The Avengers*.

The film *Avengers Assemble* was released in 2012, bringing together Iron Man, The Hulk, Thor, Captain America, Black Widow and Hawkeye.

QUESTIONS

What was the name of the coffee shop in the first image? *(page 7)*

Where did Jack follow the girl in the red hood to? *(page 8)*

How many heroes are there in the League of Enchanted Heroes? *(page 10)*

What had Jack's chewing gum been replaced with? *(page 22)*

Who is your favourite enchanted hero?

MEET THE AUTHOR

Tim Collins has written over 50 books for children and adults, including *Wimpy Superhero*, *Cosmic Colin*, *Monstrous Maud* and *Dorkius Maximus*.

His other titles for Badger Learning include *Mr Perfect*, *Joke Shop* and *The Black-Eyed Girl*. He has won awards in the UK and Germany.

MEET THE ILLUSTRATOR

James Lawrence hails from a faraway land of vikings and motorcycles. He spends his days drawing rad pictures and chugging ice tea.
He is the creator of the fantasy wrestling webcomic *The Legend of La Mariposa*.